Snap!

Written and illustrated by Charlotte Middleton

Collins

I do like your ...

pretty spots

bright feathers

curly tail

shiny teeth

long trunk

Ideas for reading

Written by Clare Dowdall, PhD
Lecturer and Primary Literacy Consultant

Learning objectives: children read and understand simple sentences; they answer 'how' and 'why' questions about their experiences and in response to stories and events; they make observations of animals and plants and explain why some things occur, and talk about changes; they show sensitivity to others' needs and feelings

Curriculum links: Expressive arts and design: Being imaginative; Personal, social and emotional development: Making relationships

High frequency words: I, like

Interest words: shiny, teeth, pretty, spots, bright, feathers, curly, tail, long, trunk

Resources: interest-word flashcards, pencils and papers for drawing

Word count: 47

Getting started

- Look at the front cover together. Ask children to identify the characters and the setting for this story. Challenge them to predict what might happen in this story, and why it is called *Snap!* Explain that this is a retelling of a well-known story.

- Turn to the back cover and model reading the speech bubble and the text with an expressive voice. Point to the exclamation mark and explain what it means. Ask children to read the words expressively with you.

- Using flashcards, show children the interest words. Help them to practise reading each word in turn, noticing any tricky parts and irregular pronunciation, e.g. pretty.

Reading and responding

- Turn to pp2–3. Ask children to read the text in the speech bubble aloud with expression. Support children as they read, model how to use a flattering voice. Pause to ask children to suggest what the giraffe may be thinking and feeling when the elephant speaks to her.